*This story is dedicated to all children
but especially mine.
Starting with Matt and Sarah
and extending to their amazing spouses
Tamara and Lance
and then to the grands in chronological order:
Avery, Romy and Hazel
and then of course to the man who made it all
possible — the daddy and now Pappy —
Roger!
A love story for all of them and for the readers, you!*

Avery, Sarah, Romy, Lance, Matt, Tamara & Hazel

ISBN 10: 1-934527-28-9   ISBN 13: 978-1-934527-28-3

Copyright © 2010 Torah Aura Productions. All rights reserved.

No part of this publication may be reproduced or transmitted in any form or by any means graphic, electronic or mechanical, including photocopying, recording or by any information storage and retrieval system, without permission in writing from the publisher.

Torah Aura Productions • 4423 Fruitland Avenue, Los Angeles, CA 90058

(800) BE-Torah • (800) 238-6724 • (323) 585-7312 • fax (323) 585-0327

E-MAIL <misrad@torahaura.com> • Visit the Torah Aura website at www.torahaura.com

MANUFACTURED IN MALAYSIA

Once upon a time there was a little boy, not unlike some of you. He lived with his mommy and his daddy, his grandma and his grandpa, and all his brothers and sisters. He was the oldest child in this very big place called the castle because his daddy was the king! Everybody at the castle had a job, and Grandma's job was to make cookies. Grandma was very wise and knew that one day this little boy would be king. So she used that special time to tell him stories about his daddy the king when he was a little boy making cookies. Making cookies and working together was more than just baking.

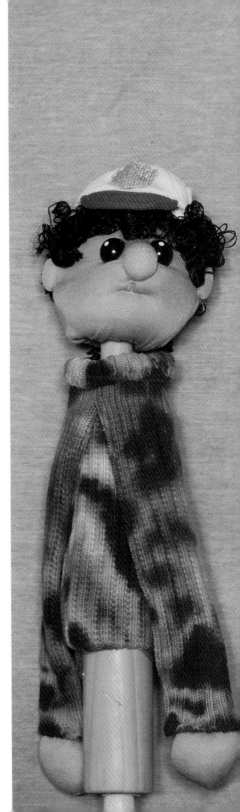

So every time she made cookies she invited the little boy. And it worked exactly as she knew it would. He loved making cookies with Grandma. They would add and stir and chop and drop and talk. After that they put the cookies in the oven, and the timer went "DING". When the cookies were done Grandma and the little boy shared them with everyone around, but the making and baking they kept just between them. Making cookies with Grandma was more than just the cookies.

Years passed, and now the little boy was the king! But, as his daddy lived to be one hundred and twenty years old. By the time he got to be king Grandma was gone, and he needed to find someone to make her cookies.

On the first Friday morning of his kingship he went into the kitchen and called for his royal chef.

"Royal chef, royal chef!"

And who should come running but the royal chef? He was the chef in charge of baking.

"What is it, Your Majesty?"

"I want cookies like my grandma made when I was a boy. Thinking of it makes me smile with excitement and shiver with delight!" said the king.

"Not a problem, Your Majesty. I am the finest baker in the kingdom, and I would be happy to oblige. But I am not your grandma, and I don't have her recipe," said the royal chef.

"I can get that for you easily," said the king. He went into his royal room and climbed up to the highest shelf in his royal closet and pulled down a dusty recipe box, and out came the recipe—spattered with ingredients and yellowed with age.

"Here it is. Don't leave anything out!" the king ordered.

This royal chef did exactly as the king asked. He added and stirred and chopped and dropped and set the timer. When the oven timer went "DING" he pulled out a beautiful tray of cookies and brought them to the king.

"Here they are, Your Majesty. Cookies just like your grandma made."

"Did you leave anything out?" the king asked.

"No, Your Majesty, I followed the recipe exactly."

The king was very excited. He took a royal sniff and bit off a piece of the freshly baked cookie. Then he chewed and swallowed and said, "This does not taste like my grandma's cookie. You left something out! Goodbye, my chef, and good luck!"

The chef had a new job the next day, but the king now needed to find a new royal chef. Fortunately, he had twenty-seven chefs. They all tried Grandma's recipe, and they all failed. When the king was down to the last chef, he was worried. He wanted so much to taste a cookie that would bring back the memory of Grandma and the memories of the way things were when he was a little boy.

Now the last chef was under a great deal of strain.

"I can do it, Your Majesty. Just give me the recipe."

He, too, added and stirred and chopped and dropped. The timer went "DING," and the chef, with a great deal of confidence, pulled out a beautiful tray of cookies. He handed them carefully to the king and said, "These, Your Majesty, will taste exactly like your grandma's cookies did!" They didn't! The king said goodbye to his last chef, and now he was really troubled. Who could make cookies for him?

help wanted!
cookie makers.
big reward.
lots of dough!
—the king

"Aha!" said the wise king. "I'll go to my people."

And he did. He put up a sign in the middle of the kingdom.

> HELP WANTED! COOKIE MAKERS.
> BIG REWARD. LOTS OF DOUGH!

Everybody tried. You did, and I did. And everybody failed. The king could not get cookies like the ones his grandma had made for him.

The king became depressed and went to where all kings since the beginning of time have gone when they are depressed. He climbed to the highest point of his tower and cried.

"I'll never taste my grandma's cookies again."

Then who should come skipping down the road right below the tower but a young person just like each of you. She was on her way to her grandma's, and guess what they were going to make? Cookies! She went every Tuesday afternoon and added and chopped and dropped and told stories with Grandma. It was her favorite thing to do.

When she walked under the king's tower and heard him crying she knew something was wrong. Kings hardly ever cry.

"What is it, Your Majesty?" she yelled up to him.

"It's the cookies, little girl. Can't you read?" bellowed the king.

"Not yet!" she replied. "But cookies aren't supposed to make you cry. My grandma's cookies make me shiver with excitement and quiver with delight!" The king, hearing those two words in one sentence (grandma and cookies), raced down the tower stairs and said, "Quick! Take me to Grandma!"

And she did. She took him by the hand and through the dark-but-not-scary woods to a small cottage covered with ivy that had sweet smells coming out of the kitchen window.

Grandma, seeing her granddaughter and her very own king, raced out of the house.

First things first, she hugged her granddaughter and then thanked the king for the very royal escort and asked, "Your Majesty, what brings you here?"

"Your granddaughter says you make the best cookies. So I have brought you something to do for me, the king."

"And what would that be?" Grandma asked.

"I have brought you my grandma's cookie recipe to make for me, the king!"

"You have, have you?" Grandma replied. "No, thank you."

"What? You can't say that. Did you forget that I'm the KING?"

"No. Did you forget that I'm the GRANDMA? You see, Your Majesty, I never use anyone's recipe but my grandma's, and she used her grandma's as well. I can't do anything else. And besides, I'm too old to try."

"But I miss her, and I thought that if I could just taste those cookies the way that she and I made them, it would bring her back in my head and my heart and my tummy," the king said sadly.

"Well," said Grandma quietly, "what if you helped me?"

"Helped you? I could do that!"

The king and Grandma went into the kitchen, and there they started to make cookies. They added, they stirred, they chopped and dropped and they told stories. She told him about his daddy the king, and he told her about how scared he was sometimes—scared that he might fail the people he loved so much.

She reminded him to always pay attention to what the people needed and to be kind. By the time they were done, the three of them—Grandma and her granddaughter and the king—were buddies.

When the timer went "DING" they took out the cookies. Grandma carefully lifted the cookie tray and handed it to the king.

He said, "But we didn't add anything different. Why should it taste better than the cookies the finest chefs made?"

She said, "Your Majesty, try it. You worked hard at it."

And he did. He broke the cookie to share with his new friends, and then he popped his piece into his mouth.

A smile broke across the king's face from ear to ear.

"Now that's a cookie like my grandma made! What did we add that made it better?"

She said, "Your Majesty, that's easy. Why, when we made cookies we made them the way I make them for my granddaughter. We made them with love. It's love that's the special ingredient!"

AND THAT'S THE TRUTH!

Cookie Recipe from the King's Grandma

No baking required

Ingredients

Tan felt, one 9" x 12" piece

Scraps of dark brown felt

Brown marker

Small amount of polyfil stuffing

glue

Directions

1. Cut two pieces of tan felt cut into 3 to 4 inch circles. The edges can be rough.

2. Sew the circles together about ¼" from edge, leaving a small open space and turn inside out.

3. Stuff with polyfil as much as you think cookies should be stuffed and hand sew the open edge.

4. Cut triangular small shapes from the dark brown felt to resemble chocolate chips and adhere with glue.

Delicious, non-fattening, gluten-free and no peanuts.

To further enhance your non-edible treats add eyeballs and let them tell the story!